# Hampstead
# the Hamster

# Hampstead the Hamster

# MICHAEL ROSEN

### ILLUSTRATED BY TONY ROSS

Andersen Press
London

First published in 2018 by
Andersen Press Limited
20 Vauxhall Bridge Road
London SW1V 2SA
www.andersenpress.co.uk

2 4 6 8 10 9 7 5 3 1

British Library Cataloguing in Publication Data available.

ISBN 978 1 78344 732 9

Printed and bound in Great Britain by Clays Ltd, Elcograf S.p.A.

# Chapter One

More than anything else in the world, Leo wanted a hamster. He knew that a hamster would make him happier than a fried egg. What? Fried eggs aren't happy! Ah, but Leo always thought that fried eggs *are* happy. He loved to hear the sound of an egg frying in the pan. *Zizzle zizzle zizzle*, went the egg, and to him that sounded like the happiest sound in the world.

So, Leo wanted a hamster so that he could be as happy as a fried egg. Not long ago, he wasn't very happy. He had been sad. But if he got a hamster, he would be happy. He knew he would. He knew that for certain.

Now the big question was whether he would get one. Christmas was coming and Dad said it was time to draw up his wishlist.

"Yes," said Leo, "I'll do that, but how will Father Christmas see the list?"

"Well," said Dad, "we have ways of letting Father Christmas know." And he winked.

*Hmmm*, thought Leo to himself, did that wink mean that Dad *did* know how to get in touch with Father Christmas, or he didn't and was just making it up? It was always hard to know with Dad.

"I could write to him," said Leo. "I'm getting good at writing."

"Or you could text him on my phone," said Dad.

"Wow! Have you got his number?" said Leo.

"Let me see," Dad said. "Hmm, contacts . . . A, B, C, D, E, F . . . hmm, Famous Five . . ."

"What?! You know the Famous Five – the children in The Famous Five books by Enid Blyton???!!!"

"Yep," said Dad, still clicking through his contacts list. ". . . Fantastic Mr Fox . . . hmm . . ."

"What?!" said Leo. "You know Fantastic Mr Fox from Roald Dahl's book?"

"Yep," said Dad, "I know a lot more people than you know about, Lee-wee."

Lee-wee is what Dad had called Leo ever since he was very small and Leo was OK about him calling him that at home, but he was forbidden – absolutely forbidden – from calling him that in front of his friends.

". . . Ah yes, here we are, Father Christmas. Right, what you need to do is tap in your list, and I'll text him."

This was exciting stuff. Leo had written out a list on a piece of paper so when Dad handed him his phone he could copy it in.

Leo hadn't spelled everything exactly right, but "spellcheck" sorted out most of these.

"Sox" came out as "socks" – that was good.

"Spider-Man outfeet" came out as "Spider-Man outfit" – that was good.

"Chocklits" didn't come out as "chocolates" which is what Leo meant, but came out as "choke bits", so they had to sort that one out.

Then Leo tapped in "Hampster" and it came out as "Hampstead" which is a place in London.

"Hampstead?" said Dad. "you mean you want to go on a trip to Hampstead Heath, that huge park?"

"No, no, no," said Leo. "I want a hamster."

"Right, hmmm," Dad said. "I'm not absolutely sure that Father Christmas does hamsters. I mean, usually he does stuff that he and his helpers make. And then, there's the sleigh whizzing through the sky. Would a hamster be happy up there? Not sure."

"Yes, yes," said Leo, getting a bit worried, "but I can try." He didn't want to get that sad feeling again.

"Sure, sure," Dad said, spotting that sad look on Leo's face. "I'm just warning you in case you get disappointed."

But Leo wasn't going to be put off. As he tapped in "hamster" with Dad's help, and sent the text off to Father Christmas, he started feeling all fluttery inside and he heard his own voice deep inside his head saying, "I'm going to get a hamster, I'm going to get a hamster . . . "

And Leo pictured himself, watching his hamster running about, kicking up the sawdust, nibbling bits of carrot, drinking water and rushing to the edge of his little home to see Leo when he came back from school.

# Chapter Two

On Christmas Eve, Leo and Dad watched TV together. They saw *The Wizard of Oz* and Leo wondered what it would be like to have a body made of straw like the Scarecrow. Then he thought of how, if he got a hamster on Christmas Day, he would put straw in his little home so that he would be comfy.

Then Leo said it was time to put out a drink and a mince pie for Father Christmas and a carrot for Rudolph.

"I don't think Father Christmas needs to have a whole mince pie," Dad said.

"What?" said Leo. "You mean you think he's like you and hates them?"

"I'm not saying that, it was just a thought that maybe Father Christmas might like a chocolate biscuit this year?"

"No," said Leo. "Mince pie."

"OK," Dad said.

"If . . . if . . . Father Christmas does bring me a hamster," Leo said, "shouldn't I leave out another carrot for him?"

"Yes, yes, that would be a great idea," Dad said. "Though perhaps Rudolph and Hampstead could share it."

"Hampstead?" said Leo. "I thought you said that was a place in London."

"Yes, you're right," Dad said. "I was getting muddled."

"Maybe, Rudolph could nibble from one end and the hamster could nibble from the other," Leo said.

"*If* Father Christmas is going to get you a hamster," Dad said. "Like I said, we just don't know. I mean, would *you* want to be a hamster whizzing through the sky on a sleigh and then getting stuffed down a chimney?"

Leo thought about this. Actually, that sounded great. He imagined a hamster peeping out from a sack on the sleigh, looking out over the whole world . . . and then diving down a chimney . . .

Leo was feeling tired now. As he went off to bed, he called out to Dad, "I know why Father Christmas is so big. It's all the mince pies he eats. He has to eat hundreds . . . no, thousands . . . no hundreds of thousands . . . no, MILLIONS!!! He eats millions and millions of mince pies."

"Don't forget to clean your teeth," Dad called out. "Father Christmas checks everyone to see if they've cleaned their teeth. If they haven't, he whizzes back up the chimney and that person doesn't get any presents."

Leo cleaned his teeth really well, hoping that the better he cleaned his teeth, the more chance he had of getting a hamster.

Then off he went to bed, saying over and over again, "I'm going to get a hamster, I'm going to get a hamster."

He thought that by saying it over and over again, that would help him get a hamster too.

# Chapter Three

Christmas morning was very, very quiet in Leo and Dad's house . . . until Leo slowly, slowly woke up.

Then he rushed into Dad's room, jumped on the bed and screamed in his ear, "Dad, Dad, Dad, Dad, Dad, Dad — let's go downstairs and see what Father Christmas has brought!"

Dad slowly levered himself out of bed, and off they went to the room with the Christmas tree. When they got to the door, Dad put his hand on Leo's arm and said, "Shhh, let's listen. If there's a hamster in there, we mustn't frighten him by bursting in and shouting."

Dad opened the door a tiny, tiny bit and they put their ears to the gap and listened.

From inside they could hear a little rustling sound. Very faint. Like something was scrabbling about in leaves.

Leo looked at Dad.

At first Leo wondered if Rudolph was still there. Perhaps Rudolph had eaten the carrot and was eating Father Christmas's mince pie – what with there being so many for him to eat.

Dad lifted up his hands and pretended to be a little animal, making sniffy noises through a wrinkled-up nose . . .

Could it be, could it be that *that* noise was . . . a hamster?

Really??

A hamster???

They pushed the door open, very, very slowly. There on the floor in front of the Christmas tree was a pile of presents. To one side was a box with little holes in it, that looked different from the other presents . . . and the rustling noise was coming from the box.

Leo rushed over and, opening the box, he saw . . . yes? No? Was it? Wasn't it? . . . Yes, it was a hamster! The most gorgeous little ginger hamster with little brown eyes that looked straight at Leo like he had known Leo all his life.

This was the best, best, *best* day ever ever ever.

"Dad, Dad, Dad, Dad – can you text Father Christmas to thank him for it?"

"Yup! Sure, right away." And Dad got his thumb working on the keypad, sending a text.

Leo wondered what it had been like for the hamster sitting in the sleigh. What had it been like whizzing down the chimney? He quickly looked at the plate where he and Dad had left the carrot – yes, the hamster and Rudolph had had a good old nibble.

Leo put his hamster in his little home and looked down at him. He looked right into his eyes, and it seemed for a moment that the hamster was asking him something, trying to tell him something, almost pleading with him for something.

Leo saw that there was plenty for him to eat and drink – no problem there . . .

What was he trying to say?

# Chapter Four

Dad said, "Aren't you going to open any of your other presents?"

"Yes, yes, right . . ." Leo said, but something was just bothering him a bit about the way the hamster had looked at him . . . and was still looking at him.

*No matter*, he thought, and went over to open the other presents — his favourite football socks, just as he had asked. And his favourite chocolates, again, just as he asked . . . and — hooray — a Spider-Man outfit. And the *Jumbo Joke Book*.

Yes! Wow, it had all worked out great. But even as he thought, *It's all worked out great*, it didn't quite feel as great as he hoped. He looked over to the hamster's little home. He was still looking at Leo with that pleading look on his face.

"Well," said Dad, "what about a name? What are you going to call him?"

Leo had a think . . . He looked back at the hamster who, to tell the truth, was not looking like the happiest hamster in the world.

Maybe, Leo thought, he should think of a name that might cheer him up . . . like . . . er . . . Hammy? Hammy the Hamster? That sounded quite cheery . . . Or what about Henry the Hamster? That sounded quite important . . . but what if the hamster was going to be naughty like Horrid Henry? He could call him Horrid Henry Hamster!

Then he remembered how the spellcheck on Dad's phone had come up with "Hampstead" and how Dad had said Hampstead the night before . . . *Hampstead the Hamster*. That sounded good and he could imagine taking Hampstead to Hampstead Heath and letting him run about in the woods . . .

"Hampstead," said Leo. "Hampstead Heath the Hamster."

"Great!" said Dad.

And they both looked at Hampstead Heath. He was still doing that pleading, begging thing, but now he was lying on one side.

They both went over to his little home.

It looked for a moment like his little paws were held together, like he was begging. And it was so sad that he was doing that.

When Leo had got dressed, Dad said, "Look, Lee-wee, you know you're in charge of little Hampstead Heath here. It's your job to keep him cheery . . . and if he's feeling sad, it's down to you to cheer him up. I can help you to start off with, so, what shall we try first? How about some food? What do you think? Here, take this straw and poke some food in front of him. Animals always like food."

So Leo did just that. He took the straw off Dad and then he poked a piece of pea that was lying there and pushed it in front of Hampstead.

Hampstead took no notice of it at all.

It wasn't looking good. Hampstead wasn't looking at all happy. Was that a little groan, Leo heard?

What could be wrong with him?

Dad said that he had to get on and get the Christmas dinner ready, and as Dad went off to the kitchen, Leo said that maybe he would tell Hampstead some of the jokes from his *Jumbo Joke Book* that Father Christmas had brought.

"Maybe Hampstead would like to hear some good jokes, Dad?"

Good one, Lee-wee. Yeah!

"What do you call a fish with no eyes?" Leo read from the *Jumbo Joke Book*.

Hampstead took no notice.

Hampstead still took no notice.

"No, I don't get that one either," Leo said. "No, hang on . . . no eyes, no 'i's . . . no letter 'i' . . . so it's 'Fssssh' with no 'i' in it, I gettit, I get it!"

But Hampstead didn't find it at all funny.

"OK, here's one:

Leo frowned again. "No, Hampstead, I don't get that one either . . . oh hang on, the doctor's ignoring him, too."

Hampstead didn't think that one was funny either. He now lay on his side, looking like someone had just told him that his favourite football team had lost ten-nil.

And so it went on until it was dinnertime and Leo got to thinking about all the things that he liked about Christmas . . . like being with Dad, and Dad singing his favourite old-school songs as he cooked. That gave Leo the idea that maybe Hampstead would like to come into the kitchen and hear Dad chuntering away with his old-timey songs. And then Hampstead could sit in his little house on the table and have Christmas dinner with them. Great idea!

So, Leo took Hampstead's home into the kitchen, near to where Dad was opening and closing the oven, tutting to himself that he had forgotten to turn the potatoes over, while he sang his old faves.

Yes, that did seem to cheer up Hampstead a little. He seemed to like being part of what was going on. And when Leo poked a Brussels sprout into his little home, he even had a nibble.

Even so, it wasn't long before Hampstead went back to staring at Leo and Dad with those begging, pleading, imploring eyes. Was that now a little tear in his eye? Oh dear, it really seemed like it.

What could it be? What was the matter?

# Chapter Five

After dinner, Leo and Dad went back into the sitting room, taking Hampstead with them. They played quizzes, asking each other hard questions.

Leo asked Hampstead some too:

"Sniff!" went Hampstead.

"Right!" said Leo, but being right first time didn't seem to cheer him up either.

Just then Leo noticed that there was another little parcel tucked under the tree that he hadn't opened.

"Hey Dad," he said, "I haven't opened that one." And he went over and picked it up. As he did so, Leo noticed that Hampstead perked up and rushed to the edge of his little house, almost as if this parcel could be for him.

Leo opened it. It was a mug with Leo's name on it and it had a picture of Leo and an arrow pointing towards Leo's face and a sign saying, *Leo's mug.*

"Why does it say that?" Leo asked.

"Ah yes," Dad said, "'mug' is a funny word for 'face'. So it's a mug *and* it's a 'mug'. Do you get it? Yes? No? Do you get it?"

"Kind of," Leo said.

"This is my mug," Leo said to Hampstead, pointing at the mug.

Hampstead didn't get the joke either.

And now, after the little moment when he had perked up, he fell back into a slump, his few seconds of hope all gone.

Leo looked from Hampstead to his mug and back to Hampstead.

*Oh, I get it now*, he thought, *it's my mug and it's got my "mug" on it.* He smiled. It felt good to have a present he had forgotten. Another present. *The presents this year have made me sooooooooo happy.* He paused. *Presents! That's it!* he thought. *That's what's wrong with Hampstead!*

# Chapter Six

Leo shouted to Dad. "Dad! Dad! Dad! You don't suppose, you don't suppose . . . that Hampstead's fed up because he didn't get a Christmas present? What do you think?"

Dad immediately stopped thinking up new quiz questions.

"Leo, you know, you could be right. I didn't think of that."

"Right," Leo said, "so couldn't we do it? Give him a present? Like, we could wrap a carrot, write a label, 'For Hampstead' and put it in his little house."

"Good one," said Dad. "Let's do it."

So that's what they did. Leo did the wrapping and wrote on the label:

And they put it in the little house.

For a moment again, Hampstead perked up. He scampered over to the little parcel of carrot but then seemed to stop in his tracks . . . as if it wasn't quite right . . . as if something was missing. He looked back at Leo with his longing, pleading, begging, nearly-crying eyes.

It wasn't right.

Dad and Leo looked at Hampstead. It was all beginning to look very sad.

Then Leo said, "No, hang on, Dad, hang on. You know what, Dad? We didn't ask Hampstead what he wants. We just went right on ahead and gave him a carrot. With me, I texted Father Christmas, didn't I? That's how Father Christmas knew what presents I wanted. Well, it's too late for that now, Father Christmas must be back in bed by now, eh?"

"Go on," said Dad, listening very carefully to what Leo was saying.

"We've got to ask Hampstead what he wants."

"Ye-es," Dad said a bit doubtfully.

So now Leo went right up close to Hampstead's house and said very slowly and quietly, "Hampstead? Hampstead? Do you want a present?"

Hampstead lifted up his head and sniffed.

It looked so much like he was saying, "Yes."

"Hampstead?" Leo went on. "Can you show me what you would like?"

Hampstead twitched his ears and twitched his nose, like he was really, really thinking. And then, he stood up and did a kind of running-on-the-spot thing. It was like he was scampering really fast but staying in the same place.

Dad watched. He looked at Leo and shrugged as if to say, "I can't figure that one out." But Leo watched Hampstead, his eyes focusing as hard as he could on what Hampstead was doing, running with his little feet in the sawdust on the floor of the house.

"I've got it!" shouted Leo. "I've got it. Dad, don't you get it? You see what he's showing us. He wants one of those wheel things! You know, the ones that hamsters get into and belt round and round in for hours on end. He wants one of those. And he's just told me."

They looked back at Hampstead. He had stopped running on the spot. And now he was looking first at Leo, then at Dad, as if to say, "Have you got the point, now, you two? I wanted a present. You got that. But then you just gave me a bit of old carrot. I didn't ask for a carrot. Then you got it again. You hadn't asked me what I wanted. Right. So then I showed you I wanted a wheel. And you got that? So, come on guys, it's Christmas. Get me a wheel, OK?"

# Chapter Seven

"We've got to do it, Dad, " Leo said.

"What?" Dad said.

"Make Hampstead a wheel."

"A wheel? A wheel? Now?"

"Yes, look at him, he's getting sad again."

And, sure enough, Hampstead had dropped his head back on to the floor and was looking back up at them, with such a pleading, begging look in his eyes.

"You know, Dad, we could just go into the shed and find stuff and make one."

Dad laughed. The shed! Yes, the shed was what he called his "Treasure Trove", a place where, for the last twenty years, he had put any old nail, screw, bracket, cog, wheel, pump or spring that he hadn't used at work. There were hundreds of bits and pieces in there.

Leo grabbed Dad by the hand and lugged him off to the shed.

"Won't be a moment, Hampstead," Leo called as they disappeared out of the room.

It was cold in the Treasure Trove, and the old bits of metal felt even colder. They both got to work, looking for bits that could make a wheel that Hampstead could get on and run on, while, well . . . staying in the same place.

Dad was muttering things about:

Leo was ignoring him, and kept pulling things off the old dusty shelves, saying,

None of this was right until they found one bit of old metal junk that looked a bit like the tray of pickles that Hakim usually brought them at the New Bengal restaurant. Each pickle was in a little cup and you spun the tray round to get to the next pickle. Leo's favourite was the mango chutney, but once he had tried the lime pickle and it felt as if his face nearly exploded.

"What about this?" Leo said and spun the tray-thing round.

"You've got it!" Dad shouted enthusiastically. "You've got it, Lee-wee!"

Dad took it off Leo and immediately started unscrewing things and tying other bits to it, and digging out nuts and bolts and all sorts.

Leo loved it when Dad was in this sort of a mood, really getting on with something while Leo helped him.

After about half an hour of all this tinkering around, Dad said, "I think this is it. Let's give it a try, Lee-wee!"

So they came out of the shed and went back to where Hampstead was waiting for them.

# Chapter Eight

The moment they walked in, Hampstead leaped up, and rushed over to the edge of his little house to meet them. Dad went to step closer to Hampstead's house but the moment he tried to, Leo stopped him and pushed the wheel out of Hampstead's sight.

"What's the matter?" Dad said. "I thought we were—"

"Shh," Leo whispered. "It's Christmas! It's supposed to be a surprise, remember? We never know for sure we're going to get what we asked for."

"Right," Dad whispered back, "got you."

So Leo pushed Dad out of the room whispering, "We've got to find some nice wrapping paper, and a nice shiny label . . ."

They groped around at the bottom of a cupboard and dug out some really glossy wrapping paper, all gold and shiny. And they found a label saying: *FOR* and *LOVE FROM* on it.

They wrapped the wheel thing, and stuck it together with some special Christmassy tape that had holly and berries on it.

"Hey, Dad," said Leo, "you don't think Hampstead will think this is real holly and try to eat it?"

"He's not daft, is he, your hamster?" Dad said, laughing. "Remember, he knew how to ask you for a wheel, so he's not going to chew up some plastic tape telling himself it's a lovely bunch of holly!"

Dad handed Leo a pen. Very carefully, Leo wrote in the spaces:

FOR Hampstead Heath the Hamster. Open this parcel and you will have a wheely good time LOVE FROM Leo and Dad. x

"*Wheely* good time, Dad. You get it?"

"No," Dad said. "What's it mean?"

"'Wheely' because there's a wheel, but it sounds like 'really', see? Get it?"

"No," Dad said and then he couldn't stop himself from laughing.

"You *did* get it. You did get it!" Leo said. "You were just trying to trick me."

"Yup," said Dad, "and I did trick you. For about one second!"

"Come on, then," Leo said. "Let's give it to him quick before anything bad happens to him."

Together they walked towards Hampstead's house, opened the special wide door in the top and lowered the wheel down inside.

Straight away, Hampstead knew what to do: he bit into the packaging, pulling it off until the wheel stood before him in the middle of his home.

Then, without waiting another second, he jumped onto the wheel and immediately raced away as fast as his little legs could go.

*Wheeeeeeeeeeeee!* went the wheel.

Was that Hampstead shrieking out a "Wheeeeeeeeeeeee!" and a "Whoooopeeeeeeeee", Leo wondered. Yes, he was pretty sure that *was* Hampstead, his very own hamster, shrieking like that.

"Wow!" said Dad. "You were so right, Leo. He wanted a Christmas present! And what he wanted was a wheel!"

Leo felt so proud and so happy. In fact, he felt as happy as a fried egg. And looking up at Dad and looking into the little hamster house at his very own Hampstead Heath the Hamster, they both looked as happy as fried eggs too.

It was definitely the best, best, best Christmas ever.